"Wrath James White's poems are red and wet love songs to a pillory, set to the beat of a flogging whip—the kind of sweet nothings Barker's Cenobites would whisper. *If You Died Tomorrow I Would Eat Your Corpse* is full of blood and sex and viscera. There are no safe words here."

—Bracken MacLeod, author of *13 Views of The Suicide Woods* & the Bram Stoker Award nominated novel, *Stranded*

"An exquisite collection exploring the lubricious carnality of love, lust, and the nightmarish pleasure of being human."

—Jessica McHugh, author of *The Train Derails in Boston*

"If Bataille had had an Instagram, if de Sade had met Clive Barker at a bus stop and gone back to his place, if you think art is not about making friends and Love is not about coming home alive, this is a book for you. At the bottom of all that blood, there's a tenderness."

—Cooper Wilhelm, author of *Dumbheart/Stupidface*

"It will leave you raw and dripping."

—Amber Fallon, author of *The Warblers*

# IF YOU DIED TOMORROW I WOULD EAT YOUR CORPSE

## YOUR CORPSE

*Poems of the erotic, the romantic, the violent, and the grotesque*

### WRATH JAMES WHITE

# INDEX

Introduction: Poems to Fuck to      ix

Untitled      1
It's A Rainy Day      2
The Milk of Human Depravity      7
Cupid in Bondage      9
Our Sick Declining Years      11
Inside      12
Crimes of Passion      13
The Taste of Your Pain      15
In Passion's Name      16
Facial      17
The End of It All      18
Flowers of Eros      19
Womb      20
Her Nightmare      21
This Is My Blood      28
Cuddling Her      29
Torso      30
Sickening      31
At the Dinner Table on Christmas Day      33
Until the Next Time      34
When Nightmares Fade      36
Edible      37
Remainder      38
She Wolf      39
The Making of Me      40
The Death of Passion      41
Astral Projection      43
Perpetual Motion      45

Just Like Whores                          59
Untitled #2                               61
Untitled #3                               62
Sex & Slaughter                           63
The Last Cabbage Patch Doll               65
Ownership                                 68
The Murderer You Wanted                   69
The Death Throes of Summer                71
Humanity                                  73
This Cruel Joy                            74
Bleeding for You                          75
Haunted                                   76
Make Love to Me                           77
One Thousand                              79
Yesterday's Altar                         81
Insomnia                                  82
Memories                                  83
Sympathy for Frankenstein                 85
Beautiful Demons                          86
Sometimes                                 87

About the Author                          89

# INTRODUCTION: POEMS TO FUCK TO

I wrote many of these as love poems to my beautiful wife. Some were written when we were only dating. Some after a few years of marriage. They are odes to her, expressions of my love, lust, and affection. But, I warn you, these are not the tender verses one recites while cuddling beneath a starlit sky. These are not fond remembrances of strolls on the beach or long summer drives to nowhere. These are expressions of raw, bleeding, passion. These are poems to make angry, rapturous, sensuous, violent love to. These are the words one recites in one's head while wielding a whip, while being chained to the bed, while being pounded into the mattress, while your head bangs against the headboard, while you bite the pillow and unleash muffled screams between orgasms. These are poems to spank, and paddle, and whip, flog, bite, scratch, choke, and fuck to. And that's just the nice ones.

Some of these are the poetry of violence and mayhem. Poems to crack skulls to. The music of bloody knives and swollen knuckles. They are the wails of banshees. The screams of the damned.

Why can't I just write normal love poems? Why do they have to be so sick, and brutal, and nasty? Well, I am a horror author first and foremost. My creative instincts naturally gravitate toward the darkness in life. I am also a tragic romantic.

I was hurting when I met my wife. I had only been divorced for two months, and I was dating—unsuccessfully. See, I had created a list of all the things I wanted in a woman. This was my list of "non-negotiables," the things I absolutely had to have in a relationship, things like affection, understanding, romance, intelligence, logic, a love and appreciation of art and literature, particularly horror literature, and a love and appreciation of sex, wild, kinky, deviant sex. In pursuit of a woman like that, I was going on as many as six dates a week. Those dates usually ended with me walking some nice young lady I had met on an internet dating site to her car, after a cup of coffee or two, and politely explaining that I did not plan to pursue this further, but that I wished them luck. Finding another kinky, athletic, free thinking, liberal, atheist, horror fan, in the middle of the Bible Belt, was proving to be surprisingly difficult. Then, at my very lowest moment, I met the woman who would be my wife. She contacted me through a dating website, and we went on our first date the very next day. A week later, I was telling her that I loved her. Two years later, we were married. In between, we discovered things about love and passion, the exchange of power, pleasure, and pain, that would change our lives forever. If you read in between the verses, you can catch a glimpse of our romance. But, I warn you, ours is a fire that burns brightest in darkness, and these are some dark verses indeed.

As a fan of very strict meter, the poetry in this book tends toward Japanese poetry, styles such as haikus, chokas, and bastardizations thereof. You'll notice a lot of poems that follow the chokas' open-ended 5-7-5-7-7 pattern, even when clearly not traditional Japanese poems. And some that stray slightly from that pattern with an occasional four or eight syllable line. Still others are completely free-verse, following no discernible pattern. One or two even rhyme, and there's even a Byronesque poem in iambic pentameter.

Not all of these are about love and sex. They aren't all love letters to my wife. Some of what follows, are angry missives scribbled during my miserable second marriage and the ensuing divorce. So, you'll have to forgive me if my rage comes out in less than subtle ways in these pages. Some are even older, penned during my angst-ridden youth when I found fault in everything that walked on two legs. A few, are just glimpses into my darkest imaginings, my kinks, perversions, and deviant fantasies. And, of course, some are just written for fun, drawing on iconic horror imagery as allegories for the madness I see all around. And, to round out the collection, there are a couple delicious little short stories. One, a dark erotic tale of BDSM and occult magic. The other, a tale of loves found and lost.

These are my fears, my joys, my pleasure, my pain. Enjoy.


Wrath James White July 4th, 2017, somewhere in Texas.

Pity the werewolf
what maddening lust it must feel
living among prey

1

# IT'S A RAINY DAY

I'm at work today

The skies are a rolling stew of dark clouds.

It is beautiful in its way.

Brilliant blue-white arteries of electricity rip through the gray
followed by a sound like mountains colliding.
Rain pounds the asphalt in a steady deluge
flooding the streets with murky fast-moving rivers of brown
effluence.
The dampness seeps into my bones and makes me shiver.

The somber colors have a somnolent effect
like a shot of brandy in your evening tea.

I should be at home right now,
In bed right now,
With you right now.

I'm thinking about the feel of your hips
your ass
your thighs
so deliciously soft and supple
squeezed in my hands
clenched between my teeth.
Inhaling your clean, dry, fresh-linen scent
like new babies.

My baby

I imagine cuddling against you
spooning with you
your ass pressed against my cock.

And
you
feel
so
good.

My erection swells
throbbing against you
until
I
have
to
get
inside
of
you.

My face
in the crook of your neck

kissing the artery along your throat
biting the back of your neck
like a mating lion
as I slide into your warm wetness
with urgent, indelicate thrusts
Biting your shoulder
and thrashing in a feeding frenzy,
tearing at your skin and muscle
growling
pounding my cock against your cervix
like a battering ram in a drug house raid.
A horde of demons at heaven's gate

I grip your throat in one hand
I squeeze and hear you gasp
I hear you choke
and my erection thickens
Your pain is wonderful
I let out a roar
as the pleasure begins to overwhelm me
and I let it all go
Let my civilized self
just fall to the side
and the beast emerge
riding the waves of pleasure to a place of savage lust
I am ferocious in my rapture
biting
choking
spanking your lovely ass and hips
Leaving livid red handprints
on your buttercream skin
I hear you grunt and moan
heroic in your suffering
as I pillage your sex
thrusting with reckless aggression.

I slide out of you
Slide down your body
Between your thighs
And devour your delicate flower
licking and sucking
fucking you with my tongue
attacking your clitoris
in rapid flicks
that make you moan and quiver.

You cry out
your body tensed and trembling
before you call out my name
weeping tears of satisfaction
trying to push me away
while I lick greedily at your sweet sex
and drink deep of your little death

I finally release you.

Daddy's turn.

You take my cock between your lips
ease it down deeper
swallowing every inch
until your lips are buried in my pubic hair
I feel your tongue swirling around the head
my full length throbbing in your throat
Your head rises and falls
sliding up and down my shaft
Your hands stroke me
You take your time and make it last
varying your speed
bringing me close then slowing down

When I cum
you swallow every drop
and smile at me
knowing I am pleased.

It's A Rainy Day ...

And I wish I was fucking you right now.

# THE MILK OF HUMAN DEPRAVITY

Holding the wolf to your tit
it suckles
snuggles in your warmth
your scent
of lavender and sex

You stroke and caress
its downy fur
it growls and chews
your gumdrop nipples
drinks from the milk
of human depravity
as you feed the feral beast
within you

It will grow hungrier
it will need meat
flesh
blood
it will learn
how violent we humans can be

and it will long
for the wild
we civilized monsters
deprived it of

And it will long
for the savage instinctive
unconditional love
we civilized monsters
are incapable of

# CUPID IN BONDAGE

Inside my hand
a leather strap
fifty times
across your back
just to see if you can writhe
as sexy as you dance
to see if your screams
are more honest
than your words

Between my teeth
a razor blade
shallow cuts
that heal and fade
just to see if you can learn
to love the pain
to see if you can
ever
trust again

Shackled to the bedpost

straining against your bonds
just to show you that the world
is not your friend
to prove to you
that love
is not a game

# OUR SICK DECLINING YEARS

For forty mad years
I've waited for the world's end
for the black sun's dawn
shadows burned into concrete
that endless winter
Now, the imminent decay
of this insane orb
makes me want to hug the earth
take it to my bed
fuck it gently for hours
and spawn new babies
of a more civilized breed
to nurture us both
in our sick declining years
when everything turns to shit

# INSIDE

Tasting your essence
licking from the inside out
drooling your juices
chewing my way into you
and back out of you
sucking you from my fingers
like white chocolate in the sun

# CRIMES OF PASSION

She expired with a scream
that petite morte
a shudder
and a smile
a sigh
like the exhausted breath of day
collapsing into night
pain
morphing slowly
into rapture
slipped out between
her clenched teeth
tears
like crystalline blood
from an ectoplasmic artery
dribbled
down
her
cold
white

cheeks
I kissed away her frigid tears
kissed her trembling lips
and closed her sorrowful eyes
forever

# THE TASTE OF YOUR PAIN

I miss the torture
the sweet nectar of agony
the tears of your joy
I miss your soft moans
the honest pain in your eyes
your cherubic face
smiling with bloodstained canines
exchanging power
to bond more powerfully
trading agony
to bond our souls eternal
one thousand lashes
for all the pain you would know
one thousand lashes
for all the pain you would cause
yet still the bond fades away
like the welts and weals
on your lovely ass
proving that nothing ever lasts
except the taste of your pain
remembered and cherished

# IN PASSION'S NAME

In sin, mankind becomes like the angels
our vice, the equal of their pure virtue
What vile and beautiful demons we are
in playgrounds of semen, piss, shit, and blood
hungry puppies lapping at the marrow
chewing and clawing for the sustenance
that feeds and nurtures our perverse passions
satiating our hunger between thighs
and the dripping swollen heads of eager cocks
fucking all the mystery out of love
sucking out the magic from creation
In passion's name, what sins we do commit
to sunder fragile sensibilities
and scandalize all of humanity
for one more writhing spurting orgasm
we would damn the entire universe

## FACIAL

I want to know you
so much more intimately
from the inside out
to snuggle deep within you
nestled by your heart
hearing its lonely echo
vibrate against me
Strip away the masquerade
of your supple skin
wear it like a warm blanket
and smile from behind your face

# THE END OF IT ALL

Hugging your dry bones
I drink in your putrescence
savoring your rot
your final fading essence

Yet still my lusts
Never wane, ebb, or fade
I never let go
even as you decay

My living dead lover
completely devours me
once again, we're together
as it forever must be

# FLOWERS OF EROS

Beautiful bruises
Red, purple, and blue flowers
blooming on your skin
nurtured by spanks from my hand
striking your pale flesh
I watch the flowers blossom
so very pretty
Hematomas slowly swelling
engorged as I am
Your ruptured capillaries
the stems of roses
The wet copper-scented splash
of your dripping blood
Our own erotic garden
like a playground in Eden

# WOMB

Within the vacuum
Yelling, flailing in darkness
Grasping for substance
I tumble down that dark hole
deep inside of you
and rip it open wider
so only I can fill it

# HER NIGHTMARE

Sheila had a nightmare. A black and brutal nightmare that shook her to the root of herself and left her raw and exhausted, exposed. Her identity, her womanhood, her very personhood, shattered and remade in an image she scarcely recognized. Everything she'd believed to be true of herself had been so effortlessly swept aside by the power of this dark dream it left her staggered and unsteady, unsure of her place in the world. When the morning came in sighs and moans, joints popping, bruises singing out in pain, dragging reality behind it like a beaten foe, she feared it as much as she'd feared and longed for the evening that preceded it.

The nightmare visited her every weekend—and today was Friday, nearly night time. He would be there soon. Preparing for His arrival was a ritual that calmed her in some ways yet increased her anxiety in others. Showering, oiling and powdering herself, taking her hair down from whatever do she'd styled it in to let it spill across her shoulders, lubing her asshole and sliding in the silver butt-plug He had given her, pulling the suitcase full of toys from the closet and laying out His favorite items. Sheila shuddered as she lovingly stroked the heavy flogger with the thick braided falls ending in heavy steel rings, her favorite toy, then placed it on top of the dresser beside the bed. Her back still bore the scars from the last time they'd used it.

In the days between visits from her nightmare, Sheila found it hard to concentrate on the mundane minutia of life. It was all bland, tasteless, colorless, and odorless in comparison to the intense kaleidoscope of sensations that bombarded her from the moment He set foot upon her threshold. The nightmare she lived on the weekends had more substance to her than the emails piling up in her inbox at work, the meetings with her clients and fellow employees, the casual chit chat in the office break room, whatever nonsense was on TV, even the picture of her infant son on the bureau where it had sat since his funeral one year ago, right beside his ashes. Her nightmare even made that memory less real, less heartbreaking. It didn't just help her forget. Like heroin to a junkie, rather than merely masking the pain, it made her not care about it, not care about anything but the high. His cock, His brutal hands, His teeth, His tongue, were her addiction, and she didn't give a fuck about anything else.

It was after 9 pm when the doorbell rang. The sun had bled its last fiery rivulets of arterial red across the darkening sky hours ago, and now all remnants of the day were gone. The night was solid and absolute. He never came during the day, one of the many reasons she thought of Him as her nightmare. He was the dark dream that made her scream out in the night. He stood in her doorway, almost 6'6" tall, bald, lean, hard muscles, goatee, skin the color of the evening sky, wearing black denim jeans with a thick leather belt she'd felt many times across her ass and thighs, black leather boots she'd knelt and kissed and polished with her tongue more times than she could recall, and a leather vest without a shirt. He smiled at her and growled low in His throat. She knew what that growl meant, and her sex responded with a gush, preparing for His salacious intrusion.

"Come here, Baby."

That's what He called her. Never Sheila. Baby was her name as far as He was concerned, and He was Daddy. The transgressive nature of those titles made every deviant act they performed feel dirtier, more obscene. You weren't supposed to call the man who ordered you to put a Hello Kitty butt-plug in your ass to prepare it for his cock your "Daddy." That was the title reserved for the one who raised you. But this nightmare had supplanted the man whose seed gave birth to her. This one was both more patient and loving, and more brutal and terrifying.

Sheila melted into His embrace, allowing herself to relax, give in, submit, even knowing the pain was soon to come. That was the nature of their horrible romance. That was the nightmare. Love and pain, affection, orgasm, and anguish. Endorphin rush followed by exhaustion. This was their ritual. Sheila knew it well. Enough to both fear and crave it.

Her nightmare stepped into her home, taking Sheila by the hair and pulling her after Him. He shut the door behind Him, then pushed her face against the wall. Cold, hard, hands snatched the butt-plug from Sheila's ass with less gentleness than the act required, but gentle was not His way. Moments later He was pushing His cock inside her with even less tenderness, fucking her asshole violently, grunting and growling into her ear. He reached around with one hand to squeeze her nipple, and the other to rub her clitoris. Her nightmare knew all her erogenous realms and worked them expertly to bring her to orgasm. He had three of His long, thick, fingers deep inside her, fucking her, while His thumb flicked back and forth across her engorged clitoris and He battered her asshole with His cock.

"Oh, Daddy! Oh, Daddy it hurts! It hurts, Daddy!"

Sheila's nipples ached from His pinching and twisting, but they both knew she wasn't complaining. This was exactly what she wanted, what she needed. She gasped and moaned, then cried out when He bit the soft spot on the back of her neck and thrashed His head back and forth as if trying to rip a chunk out of her. He didn't let go, continuing to thrust deep within her while holding her in place with His bite like a mating lion. He squeezed her nipple once more, hard, twisting and tugging so brutally it brought tears to Sheila's eyes, then He wrapped His hand around her throat and began to squeeze, cutting off her air as He sped up the rhythm of His thrusts, slamming her hard against the drywall.

"Oh, my God! I'm cumming, Daddy! I'm cumming!"

Daddy. There was that word again. She felt perverse and degenerate for using it. But saying it made her cum even harder.

Her climax came in spastic jerks and convulsions, bucking like a wild horse. When her nightmare's orgasm arrived, it was with a booming roar that shook the room. He withdrew His cock from her ass and forced her to her knees to receive His seed like a sacrament on her outstretched tongue, bathing her lips, cheeks, chin, breasts, in splashes of hot semen. He stroked himself back to full erection in seconds, then forced His cock between Sheila's lips, down her throat, past her tonsils, fucking her throat with as much force and urgency as He'd fucked her tight little ass. Sheila gagged, choked, and wept, but when her beautiful ebon nightmare came again, she swallowed every drop eagerly, even those spilled from her lips onto the tile floor. She knelt and lapped them up like a puppy, then did the same to the random drops that splattered His boots before slurping it from her fingers. Those were the rules. Every time He came, she was to swallow ever drop, no matter where it landed. *Waste not my seed upon the ground.* But this was just foreplay. Now the pain would start.

He dragged Sheila by her hair. She scrambled on her hands and knees to keep from having her hair yanked out by the roots. He pulled her onto the bed, across His lap, and began to spank her with His hard, calloused, hands, reddening Sheila's ass cheeks. He would pause between strikes to gently rub her bruised buttocks, kiss them lovingly, or bite them savagely. Sheila loved it all. By the time He laid her down on the satin sheets and picked up the heavy flogger, Sheila was already deep into subspace, shivering with a rush of adrenalin and endorphins.

She felt drunk, riding high on dopamine, as her beautiful ebon nightmare swung the heavy flogger with two hands down onto her back, ass, and thighs, again and again, turning His hips and shoulders to put His entire might into each blow like He was driving railroad spikes. The impact of the blows stole her breath and bruised her skin. The pain intensified as He swung it harder and harder, striking the same bruised flesh again and again until it split open and ran red and her screams reached a crescendo that threatened to shatter her soul. But, just before she broke, a wave of calming pleasure came rolling over her as her body released a deluge of endorphins. Sheila cooed and purred, high on dopamine.

She smiled up at her Daddy, her Dominant, her Master, her nightmare, as He continued to exert Himself in the brutal-ization of her. His body glistened with sweat, and not for the first time Sheila wondered what He got out of this? It took so much effort to bring her to this point of bliss, but once she was there, it was heaven, like no other high on earth, and she'd tried them all. But what did He feel? What was His reward for this effort?

As her back and buttocks ruptured and bled all over her sheets, Sheila looked into the hollow pits where her nightmare daddy's eyes should have been, where flickering shadows slithered like a nest of black eels, and could see nothing to answer her. From the day she'd first summoned Him from the pit, awakened Him from the locked tomb in which He'd been imprisoned by one god or another, all He'd ever expressed was His appetite for, and total dominance over, her. He'd used her in ways she would have never allowed any mortal man to, and she'd loved it all. The ecstasy He brought was a heaven and hell worth every sacrifice—even the one that had come from her womb.

Sheila remembered the day she'd finally walked out on her weak, impotent husband after years of unsatisfying sex. He had begged her not to go, his limp four-inch cock dangling between his legs, still wet with her juices and his own premature ejaculation. That was the last night she would ever spend with a man who could not satisfy her. She made that vow, then sealed it with an incantation and the blood of her infant son spilled over an ancient tomb. That was six years ago to the day. When her nightmare began. Tonight was her last night. Her last evening of ecstasy before her final payment was due.

The flogger fell again and again. The metal rings felt like razors as they cut into her skin. Then He removed another flogger from His toy bag. This one was braided as well, but thinner, lighter. Instead of metal rings it had barbs woven into each fall. When He swung it, the barbs hooked into her skin. He had to jerk it free, taking chunks of her with it, flaying her to the bone. She began to scream again.

"No! No, Daddy! Please!"

He swung the flogger again and again, tearing and ripping skin, fat, muscle, down to her organs and bones. Her vertebrae were exposed, the white bone visible through the torn flesh and splatted blood. Even her lungs were visible through her ribcage as she rapidly inhaled and exhaled.

"Please, Daddy! Please! Please, don't stop!"

And He wouldn't, not until every ounce of flesh was gone. Not until she was nothing but blood and bones. And then He would continue flogging her naked soul for all eternity.

# THIS IS MY BLOOD

I give communion
Spill thick upon her tongue
Slither down her throat

My lust
Like bile
Scalding her esophagus
Burning deep within

I coat her lovely face
Her engorged breasts
Her perfect ass

I empty myself
Into her
Onto her

I become her faith
And boil in her belly
With the other parasites

# CUDDLING HER

Spooned in my embrace
So little I could crush her
Squeeze her tiny form
Warm and naked against me
Still hard inside her
Exhausted and satisfied
Holding her so tight
Her breath comes as a whisper
Until hers and my
heart
stops

# TORSO

She was just a torso.
No arms to hold me,
barely more
than bleeding stubs
amputated at the shoulder
No voluptuous hips
or sumptuous thighs
just jagged ivory shards
jutting forth from her pelvic bone.
No lips to kiss.
Barely more
than teeth
without tongue
or throat.
Yet still shrieking
and cursing
and shouting.
No breasts to suckle and caress,
just bony ribs
and the empty cavity
where her heart had been.

# SICKENING

You are Gorgeous to the point of lustful excess
A horrible exaggeration of comeliness
Irresistible as thunder
Beauty
a pregnant tumor
breeding wildly in your cells
grimace quantities of sensuality
too expansive to be contained
by flesh or spirit
You are gross with it
hideously engorged
bloated
with a loveliness so profound
as to be oppressive
a weight
bending your features
into abominable perfection
Sensuousness bubbles up out of you
a sweet unctuousness
oozing from your pores
permeating your clothes

the air around you
pooling at your feet
thick and syrupy
And I would lap it from your toes
like a thirsty dog
lick it from your skin
to feel its heat
upon my tongue
rub it over my face
neck
chest
grinning
giggling
so
so pretty
Irresistible
as thunder

# AT THE DINNER TABLE ON CHRISTMAS DAY

She flashes her bruise
The impression of my teeth
A love note shared

# UNTIL THE NEXT TIME

Filthy blood-drenched dreams
Writhing in rapturous pain
From cum-stained nightmares
I awaken with a howl
That silences her.

Her corpse beside me
His vivisected remains
scattered everywhere
Meat, blood, condoms, and roses
His dead eyes watch us.

He took her from me
I took them both to hell
One victim. One lover.
Vengeance and lust consumed them.

Silence creeps like rot
building dark walls between us
imprisoning me
leaving me alone again

until the next time.

# WHEN NIGHTMARES FADE

A sexy nightmare
so turbulent in its life
ends not with a scream
but like flowers in autumn
its radiance fades
with one last exhausted sigh
as it crumbles into ash

# EDIBLE

He wants to objectify her
To reduce her endless chatter
to meat
Organs
Bones
Blood
A sweet succulent thing
he can consume
and not talk
or listen to

He closes his eyes
Inhales her vanilla skin
And takes another bite
Pain
like August sunshine
So delicious
His taste buds
Burn

# REMAINDER

I wish you could know
the love and the pain in me
I wish someone would hurt you
dare to threaten you
So I could kill them for you
I would slay legions
in defense of your honor
lay waste to worlds
heap a mountain of corpses
at your lovely feet
to build you a castle
a temple from their flensed bones
where I might worship
Until all malice vanished
and only my love remained

# SHE WOLF

A cannibal flirtation
a rattlesnake flick of the tongue
Across her meat-stained fangs
in place of a smile

Blood washes down her throat
Like warm red wine
Drools from her chin
In strawberry splatters

Her heart rages
And pushes a quivering scream
Up from her full belly
As the first orgasm
Brings her to her knees

Her body trembles still
As she licks my seed
From her carcass
And smiles
Red and meaty

# THE MAKING OF ME

I used to look
at the moon and stars
and imagine paradise

Wizened with age
corrupted by lust
I found heaven in vice

I once believed
in love and peace
and the power of prayer

But as I fought
and fucked and bled
I found God was not there

Through violence and decadence
I became what I am
In blood and sex and viscera
I emerged as a man

# THE DEATH OF PASSION

This vicious love of yours
is just another smiling corpse
mutilated and abandoned
by a society that loathes it
and all things feminine
That would see you stripped
of every sensuous curve
reduced
to a bulimic skeleton
Garishly posed
in cabaret colors
and showgirl feathers
covered head to toe
in piss and semen
eyes glued shut
vagina and rectum distended
every orifice plundered
discarded
amongst cigarette butts and beer cans
fast food wrappers and homeless tents
on the side of a busy freeway

A travesty of wasted wet dreams
and squandered lust
A parody of romance
A comedy of sin
Feeding worms and flowers
with rot and putrescence
Mushrooms growing in your waste
where your legs are splayed akimbo
displaying a formless sexless void
"She"
now a meaningless distinction
others have claimed from you
without deserving
Still trying to seduce and deceive
with no audience but strays and vermin
and leering perverts
They take the best pieces of you
to feed their loathsome offspring
become your vicarious progeny
Rubberneckers gawk as they drive past
Their own lives reaffirmed

by our tragedy

# ASTRAL PROJECTION

I dream of you
The insanity of the mind at rest
Brings me to you
When the sunlight dies
On moonlit bat wings
At the speed of night
On fast cars
With blaring horns
Screeching tires
And thundering
Radio bass
Rhythm & Blues love songs
That sing of your tears
Twinkling
On your perfect skin
I come to you
Disembodied
As spirit
To take over your flesh
Snuggle up
Close to your soul

And whisper in your heart
"I love you"
I come to you
in chains
Bruised and bleeding
And collapse at your feet
Begging you
to love me back
to love me as deeply
as I love you
I scream myself awake
And find you
Sleeping
Next to me
And you are still
My love
My flesh
My blood
My trembling soul
Is still
Yours

# PERPETUAL MOTION

Help me to avoid
the next woman
The one who comes
after you
came before you
and before her
who will lie in bed beside me
love me
tell me
about our future together
never
ever
ever
ever leave me
like you
those before you
and the next woman
the one
who will be you
when I blink

I awake, and the morning sun sears my eyes, sending a lancing pain through my skull that makes me wince and squint. I have to concentrate hard to keep from closing them completely. I slept with my eyes open all night, and my retinas are now caked with a gummy film of mucus, oil, tears, and skin cells. It forms a crust in my eyelashes. My eyes are beginning to water now. I reach out and try to wipe them clean with my fingertip. It doesn't help. Already my eyes are drying out. My tear ducts are almost empty. I try to ignore it as long as possible. I try not to blink.

I don't know how long I've been lying here with this cold clammy sweat sticking my ass to the bedspread, staring at the ceiling with that damned Lord Byron poem playing in my head like a tuneless soundtrack.

*"Yet still this fond bosom regrets while adoring/that love like the leaf must fall into the sear/that time will come on when remembrance deploring/contemplates the scenes of our past with a tear..."*

I have no idea why I'm thinking of it, or what it means in relation to my current situation, or why I haven't yet bothered to see who it is lying beside me, snoring softly. I wonder if she's someone I love, or someone I hate but love to fuck, or someone for whom I have no feeling at all and only fuck for lack of anyone better to occupy my time with.

When I first see her caramel skin, smooth slender body, and small neat afro, the hairs on the back of my neck stand up and I nearly leap from the bed. She looks so much like my mother that for a moment I think I did something really, really bad. But my mother hasn't looked like that in nearly thirty years. Besides, Mom is more of a reddish brown. More like mahogany than caramel.

I examine the sleeping woman's face meticulously. Watching the rise and fall of her dark nipples pointing skyward like little Hershey kisses, the sweet gentle smile that crosses her face as she flutters awake. She is beautiful. At least that's something.

She isn't the most beautiful woman I've known, but definitely the most beautiful one I've shared a bed with in a very long time. There have been many others. Too many. Delicate, lovely, soft, and supple, sweet, caring, and loving, fading in and out of my life like phantoms, desert mirages sent to torment a weary and dehydrated traveler, to fuel his hunger for the unattainable, like the schizophrenic hallucinations of a wino or chronic drug fiend. In the end they leave only their heart wrenching memories, pale after images, mere suggestions of substance seared into my consciousness with a scalding teardrop and the familiar tightening of the stomach that comes with the remembrance of joys never again to be enjoyed. Many of them I've cared deeply for, even loved. Too many. It only hurt that much more when they inevitably passed. Pricked by a thousand thorns for the sight and smell of a single rose. Watching each lover dissolve into the past to be replaced by the next woman.

The woman is so beautiful that I hope to God I wasn't foolish enough to fall in love with her. I can't stand another heartbreak.

*"...Yet still this fond bosom regrets while adoring."*

Her skin is like whipped milk chocolate, so fresh and clean that I can smell the water from her bath in the pores of her skin, beneath the musky aroma of sex. She has dimples and round little cheeks suspended above a smile that imprisons all innocence and softness in its pearl white cage. Her body is all long legs and break-neck curves. She reminds me of Tyra Banks or Pam Grier back in the seventies, when she starred in movies like *Foxy Brown* and *Coffy*. She has the type of voluptuous, wantonly sensual form I've always admired—no—worshipped.

*"...That love like the leaf must fall into the sear..."*

Her breasts, unlike most, seem to have a remarkable aversion to the ground. Gravity defying. They are larger than you'd ever see in the Miss America Pageant, but firmer and more buoyant than those flabby pendulous monstrosities found in magazines like "D-cup." She also has a deliciously flat stomach. I can't tell what her ass looks like because she's lying on her back. Of course, there are memories to supply that information.

There are always memories.

*"...That time will come on when remembrance deploring..."*

We met last year, although I'm sure she didn't exist until she magically appeared in my bed this morning. I was sitting on a bus, reading a book by one of those horror fiction writers who used to be really good, but have since lost the knack, yet refuse to stop bothering us with their self-imitative rip-offs that border on self-parody and we, unfortunately, refuse to stop buying them. When I looked up during a particularly weak part of the book, she was staring down at me.

"How's the book?"

It sounded like one of my "break-the-ice-quick" pick-up lines. Something I'd say right before: "Where'd you get your earrings?" Or "That's a lovely dress." Or "Are you a dancer/model/artist/actress?" I could barely stifle my urge to laugh. I thought I'd better answer before she started throwing a few of those lines at me. I closed the book making sure to save my place.

"It's not one of his best." I replied. She had the retro sixties look down. A perfectly round afro framed her face lavishly in a cushion of black wool. Huge hoop earrings dangled alongside her head, clanking noisily as the bus bounced along. Her lips were full and pouty as she blew out her words like kisses. It was amazing how much she looked and dressed like my mother did in 1973. I was freaked out by how much it turned me on.

"He doesn't seem to be trying, does he?"

"No, but I am. I'm trying to get your number. So, what's your name anyway, sweetheart?"

It was too much. I knew it right after I said it. Or rather, right after she turned on her heels and walked away. Before she retreated she let me know I had fucked up by catching my own piercing, predatory stare, that I always thought was irresistible, in her own hard dark eyes and crushing it. She threw me a more effective version of the look I'd attempted and I flinched visibly.

"My name is Lynn," she said, then turned on her platform heels and walked off down the aisle. Her mini-skirt clung to her like white on rice and her ass was truly a marvel to behold.

I stood up and started to follow her to the back of the bus when I realized she was very likely moving back there to avoid me. I might even get my ass cussed out in front of the whole bus full of rush hour commuters. I was already halfway to the back of the bus and I froze there, trying to find a way to gracefully return to my seat when some teenaged, hippie, skateboarder loaded his pot-reeking, saggy-jeaned ass into my seat, blocking my retreat.

I stared at her, trying to decide if she was genuinely interested, and reminding myself to keep my habitual sarcasm in check if I did manage to get another crack at her. A good attitude has saved as many lives as a bad attitude has lost and Lynn was a true sharpshooter, willing and able to shoot gaping holes in an ego at 500 yards in the dark. I was in eminent danger of losing points on my player card. I looked to her for help.

"Do you want me to come or not?" my eyes pleaded, but hers were ruthlessly silent.

Just as I decided that the only way for me to get out of this with my pride and players' card intact would be to act like this was my stop and simply exit the bus, she motioned for me to sit down. We had begun a battle of wills right then that ended with a circus sex marathon in the hallway just inside the door of her apartment. We had gotten ourselves so worked up that we couldn't wait to get into the apartment before we tore into each other. After an Olympian session of panting and thrusting we called our battle a draw. We've been dating ever since.

*"Yet still this fond bosom regrets while adoring..."*

Lynn rolls over and locks those hypnotic eyes on me bringing me back from my reminiscence.

"Do you love me?" she asks.

*"... That love, like the leaf, must fall into the sear..."*

I can tell by the matter-of-fact sound of her voice that she already knows the answer and is only seeking the comfort and reassurance of hearing my deep rumbling voice form the words. But I have no idea if I love this woman or not or if it even matters. My eyes are burning, and I can't possibly keep from blinking much longer.

My eyes have begun to itch irritatingly. I wonder what she thinks of the thick red veins that must be crosshatching my retinas by now? I wonder if she notices that I haven't blinked in almost ten minutes? I wonder if I love her?

From my mind comes a staggering deluge of images. Memories of moonlit walks in the park, by the river, on the beach, down deserted streets; memories of dancing 'til morning staggering around parties together drunk and giggling in each other's arms. Memories of going to a dozen different movies, plays, art openings, poetry readings. Making love in a dozen exotic places, in a dozen exotic ways, and I realize that I do love her. That's fucked up. That's real fucked up. 'Cause there's no way I can keep my eyes open much longer.

"Yes. I love you, Lynn."

"Will you love me forever?"

Unwilling to start a painful discussion of loves' ephemeral nature, I reply instead with a kiss. I kiss her with the same hungry eager passion I bring to every experience in this timeless continuum where each moment is murdered as it is conceived. Our lips touch, and I send out my tongue in search of hers. To coax it, warm and slippery, into my mouth. I reel and sway in rapture as I nip at her lips and suckle her tongue. I want to devour her, to possess her forever as an intimate part of me. But I know that cannibalism is not the answer. I'd only wake up in jail the next time I blinked and the cycle would continue, only this time with an endless series of big hairy convicts. Not at all a pleasant thought.

When we separate from our embrace, she brushes against my cheek with hers. Bringing her lips to my earlobe, she whispers softly—too softly.

"I'll love you always," she says. "We're going to have a wonderful life together." Her voice has changed.

It is no longer Lynn.

I realize that in my ecstasy I have closed my eyes. I find myself not wanting to open them. Not ever again. But the heat of the body pressed against me is crushing my resolve. A single tear drops from each eye and washes away the filmy residue that had built up on them, but unfortunately, fails to wash away the taste of Lynn's lips against mine, or the rosewood scent of her perfume.

The woman in my arms, with her face inches from mine, is black. Not caramel, or cappuccino, but gunmetal black, with long dreads decorated with seashells and little silver ornaments. Her breasts are small, but as I run my hands over her body, I find an ass the size of two of Lynn's, that sits up high on her back and jiggles pleasantly when I rub it. Her arms and shoulders are hard and muscular, and her thighs are likewise carved of some unyielding black stone. She is obviously some type of athlete.

"I'll love you forever," she whispers in a lush, smoky voice. She grinds her wetness against my manhood, causing it to leap to life and swell almost painfully erect. Before I can really get a good look at her, she disappears beneath the covers. As her lips caress my body, I notice that I've been working out in the time between Lynn and...Uh...um...Alicia. Yes. What a lovely name. My body is now ripped with muscles and her kisses fall expertly upon them. I lie back and enjoy, as she descends down my body with her mouth and tongue teasing tingles from my flesh. Still shaking from a powerful orgasm, I wait for her to rise from beneath the covers. When her face reaches mine, it is no longer Alicia.

This face I have seen before. Not in my memories or dreams, but here in this room, in this bed. We had loved each other, and I had blinked, and she was gone, like the others, but now—she's back. As if the rotation of the earth had carried her away from me and then right back again like some twisted carousel ride, a demented merry-go-round with horses going in opposite directions that meet every so often for the briefest of moments. Somehow I have to stop the ride right here, with Shana in my arms. I can't deal with the idea of losing her again.

"I love you, Shana. God, I love you! You have no idea what I've been going through without you!"

She smiles at me, rather perplexed and amused.

"What are you trippin' on?"

I just look at her, smiling through tears.

I remember how wild she used to be. She was my best friend, and we went everywhere together. She was so gorgeous, still is, in an androgynous sort of way. Her small breasts, short, dyed-blonde crewcut and aggressive mannerisms, could have easily allowed her to pass for a man. Though not the kind you'd want on your side in a fight. I can't count how many times we would get peculiar looks as we walked down the street, holding hands and kissing, by people who thought she was a dude. She didn't help the situation by getting all ghetto and yelling: "Fuck is you lookin' at fool? I'll bust a cap in your ass!" Though it usually caused them to find more interesting things to look at. That always sent us into hysterical laughter. Once, when she overheard a couple on the bus speculating about whether she was a girl or a very pretty homosexual man, she stood up and flashed her tits at them, ending the debate. Baby was pretty wild. Those were good times—very good times.

*"Yet still this fond bosom regrets while adoring..."*

I hug her to me and begin kissing her face while repeating my declaration of love over and over, like a program stuck in an infinite loop, like my entire love life, an infinite loop. Meet girl. Fall in love with girl. Lose girl. Meet girl. Fall in love with girl. Lose girl. So on and so on. Over and over. One girl after another. Ad infinitum. But not this time.

I stretch my eyelids back and prepare to fight off the inevitable. Shana smiles at the bizarre expression. But I hold it, despite the discomfort.

This time it will be different. No matter what I will not blink. I will not lose her again. I will never let my eyelids drop. No matter the pain. No matter the gnawing itchiness and irritation. I've got to hold on. I can't let Shana slip away again. This isn't just another ho I'm fucking. Shana is a friend—one of a very few. Perhaps that's why she came back when none of the others did? Maybe the carrousel has finally stopped?

*"... That love like the leaf must fall into the sear..."*

I ask her to tell me all about herself—about us, and our life together, our future together.

*"... That time will come on when remembrance deploring..."*

"You know all about me. What can I tell you?"

Of course, I do know all about her. I know that she wanted to be an actress when she was in high school, before that she wanted to be an artist, and now she designs hats and makes jewelry. I know that she was a tomboy in high school, and that she didn't get her period until she was fourteen, and didn't develop breasts until she was sixteen. I know that she lost her virginity (to me) at age eighteen, and that when she was in college she decided she was a lesbian and gained nearly twenty-five pounds saying that she no longer felt compelled to conform to male standards of beauty. I found that amusing. It seemed to imply that the true nature of femininity was obesity. When I shared this observation with her she called me every son-of-a-bitch she could think of, and punched me 'til her arms got tired, even after I'd apologized. I can still remember sitting there, hugging my battered body as I continued to apologize, laughing and being secretly amazed at how hard she could hit. I guess all that extra poundage did have its practical applications.

I remember all of it like it was yesterday. The memories are always clear as a photograph. They ought to be. They're only about a few hours old. Wasn't that when she was here last? When all those years went by? Just a few hours ago?

"Please just tell me. Act like—like we just met."

She talks into the night, pausing occasionally to ask me why I'm crying, as I struggle desperately to keep my agonized eyes wide. She designs our future home, room by room. It is an old colonial mansion complete with angels, and gargoyles, and swirling designs in hand-carved wood. The interior is black and white art deco with gray and black marble floors and large sculptures seemingly in place of furniture. She manages to engage me in a discussion on what we should name our child. After going through a few less-than-flattering suggestions (including Rusty and Dusty) we decide to name our child Pharaoh, if it's a boy. We come to the mutual conclusion that I shouldn't have a girl. Not with my Karma.

As we talk, I find myself slowly slipping into the fantasy, actually starting to believe that she is more than just an illusion resulting from all five senses hallucinating at once, actually starting to believe that she will not disappear like the rest of them. I find myself believing in the forever and ever, voicing concerns over a house, a child, a family, an entire life, that will never exist.

"I know you don't believe me, really believe me. You probably never will. But I do love you, and I'll never leave you. Never. I'm not like the others. I love you."

I don't want to tell her how many times I've heard that same statement, spoken from countless faces with eyes just as honest and sincere as hers, because this time I believe it. I believe her. Even though my eyes are twitching and itching in their sockets. I believe her even though they are burning as if someone massaged them with rock-salt and left a little tucked under each eyelid. Even though my tear ducts are empty and my eyes are so dry and tacky that I can't even see her. Even though one of my eyes has now plastered itself shut, causing her image to fade, shiver, and shift in and out, transposed with the image of the next woman. Even though I know I'm about to blink.

"Shana..."

I pull her tightly to me and we begin to make love, passionately, furiously, our bodies crashing against each other as if in battle, as if somehow she, too senses that time is short.

"No. No. No! No! Nooooooo!!! Don't leave me! Not you too! Don't leave me!!!!"

My eye feels as if it is about to explode from my head. I see the worried look on Shana's face. Then I blink. And it is over. She is gone.

I scream and blink a dozen times, hoping I can bring her back.

"Why? Oh God why? Why do they always have to go!?! Why? Why? Why?!!!"

Beneath my body, for split seconds between blinks, I see a staggering menagerie of different women appear. Plump ones, skinny ones, Black ones, White ones. One or two that look old enough to be my mother, or young enough to be my daughter. A Samoan woman with hard warrior eyes, a wide nose, and full lips like my own, who I met at a grocery store. A Nigerian woman with a shaved head who I met at a Reggae club at five o'clock in the morning. A Filipino woman with massive breasts and eyes like an abused child that I met at a shopping mall. Some of them look like Lynn. Some of them look like Shana. But they all disappear, and I feel each loss like a stabbing wound and neither Shana nor Lynn return. They are gone forever. Back into nonexistence or someone else's bed.

Finally, I stop crying. Stop blinking. Beneath me now is a woman with long black hair. Her eyes are black as pools of liquid obsidian. Her pale white skin is the unearthly pallor of a vampire's. Her lips are so red they appear to have been soaked in blood. She is inhumanly lovely. Her name is Renee'.

"How long have we been together?" I ask her, my eyes still wet with tears.

"Three wonderful years," she replies while stretching a body not half the equal of her face. She has a feint German accent. Where the fuck did I meet her?

"That's the longest I've ever been with anyone."

"I know," she purrs. "That's why you married me."

For a moment, I am too shocked to speak. I guess my traitorous face betrayed my bewilderment, because she stared at me, looking simultaneously worried and annoyed. I allow the memories to seep from my subconscious to the forefront of my mind.

It seems we met at Lynn's funeral. She'd been murdered by a jealous boyfriend after he caught her cheating on him. Renee' had been her roommate after Lynn and I parted company. Following the funeral, we'd kept in touch under the pretense of comforting each other through that terrible time. It wasn't long before we became lovers.

She was there for me when my grandmother died. She let me move in with her when I lost my apartment. She was with me to celebrate the publication of my first novel. So, when she wanted to get married and raise a family, I felt duty bound to be there for her. Today is our wedding night. I look down at the little gold band on my finger, and a weak, unenthusiastic hope, swells in my chest before flickering out forever.

*I wonder if this is the answer? Just getting married? I wonder if this will stop the carrousel? The rotation of the earth? End the infinite loop? No. No. It wouldn't—it couldn't be that easy. Ain't shit ever that easy. The merry-go-round ain't ever going to stop. It just keeps going on and on and no little ring is going to stop it. No vow of fidelity, no fucking 'til death do us part is going to freeze its gears. It just keeps going 'round, grinding my sorry black ass into the dust!*

I begin to laugh.

Again, the worried look from Renee'.

"Forever and ever," she says, then catches me staring at the ring and adds: "'Til death do us part."

This makes me laugh harder. Then I blink, and she is gone, and, for the first time, it is a relief.

"I won't open my eyes again. Not this time. Not ever again."

I imagine digging my fingers into my eye sockets and tearing my eyes out of my head. I picture myself lacerating the tendons and optical nerves with my jagged fingernails. It would be just like ripping oysters from their shells.

"I love you. I'll love you forever," I hear someone saying.

My eyes are still squeezed shut. I don't know who's lying next to me now. I don't care who it is any longer. Just as long as they stay ...

*... forever and ever ...*

"I'll never leave you," the woman says.

*... 'til death do us part.*

*No, you'll never leave me. Because I'm going to rip my eyes right out of my fucking skull and I'll never blink again.*

"Just you and me sweetness." I laugh and lick my teeth nervously.

*"Yet still this fond bosom regrets while adoring..."*

I begin to reach beneath my eyelids. I touch my eyes, and it reminds me of that Halloween game we used to play with peeled grapes when we were kids.

"This is an eyeball," someone would say while they placed the peeled grape into your hand. And it felt...just like this. But what if I rip out my eyes and this woman disappears and no one returns in her place? What then Einstein?

*"...That love like the leaf must fall into the sear..."*

"That's just a chance I'll have to take."

My fingers hook into claws.

*"...That time will come on when remembrance deploring..."*

"I'll always love you," she says.

My last thought, before I destroy my sight, is about that old movie "The Man with the X-ray Eyes!" At the end of the picture the guy goes crazy and tears out his eyes, then the screen goes blank. But rumor has it that in the original director's cut, after he rips out his eyes, he turns and screams to a horrified audience: "I can still see!"

"That's just a chance I'll have to take," I say to myself.

And then the screaming starts.

*"...Contemplates the scenes of our past with a tear."*

"I'll love you forever."

# JUST LIKE WHORES

He laughed at her fangs
And at her bloodless pallor
Who still believes in vampires?

She was beautiful
A romantic dream of death
In satin and lace

Sensuous killer
Powdered corseted bosom
Cleavage splashed with red

Her black lipstick smile
Pouting like a spoiled child
Full lips like bloated leeches

Leonine canines
Rancid like an abattoir
From her last Romeo's blood

He offered her his throat

Let her drink just a little
One small taste of life

He watched her imbibe
Grotesquely slurping
Watched it trickle from her lips

Dripping down her throat
Between her lovely pale breasts
Licking her fingers

So very lovely
His blood on her swollen lips
His first vampire

So very lovely
He would have to remember
Each salacious cut

He took her slowly
Bled her of secrets and screams
He smiled, contemplating
That vampires bled just like whores

## UNTITLED #2

Enthralled by your flesh
In love with you utterly
your body, mind, and spirit
and if you died tomorrow
I would eat your corpse

# UNTITLED #3

Love is the desire to unite
enraptured twins conjoined at the soul
My heart hungers for that physical union
becoming one with you completely
Tattooing your living flesh onto mine
wearing your meat and blood like warm clothing
your fat, muscles, organs like ornaments
knitted to my body as living art
a sensuous and gruesome second skin
face to face, chest to breasts, sex to sex
loving you as you die all over me

# SEX & SLAUGHTER

How can you say I do not love you
merely because I am destructive
in the expression of my love?

I love you
as only the starving wolf
can love the wounded deer
with an obsessive adoration
like physical hunger.

It is to adore them forever
uninterrupted
that I would pinch off your eyelids
to never be denied the spectacle
of your wondrous eyes.

It is to never see your lovely smile
deceased from your face
that I would
with fish hooks
pull up the corners

of your full red lips
and pin them to your cheeks.

It is so your voluptuous breasts
would never succumb to age or gravity
that I would bind them in piano wire
and anchor them to your throat.

And so you would never forget
the sensation of my mouth
wet hot against the joining of your thighs
and I
never to forget the taste
that I would cannibalize your sex
savage your labia and clitoris
with my teeth
chew up into your ovaries.

And how could mere malice
or cowardly misogyny
explain such an act?
Only love can rationalize this madness
this passion
which even now brings the taste of your sex
melting on my tongue like a sweet confection
to my taste buds
and tears of the most profound joy
to my adoring eyes.

# THE LAST CABBAGE PATCH DOLL

In Macy's parking lot
The snow turned red
Tom's shirt, his pants, his underwear, his socks
Tacky, sticky, red
Red pooled in his shoes as he staggered forward
Red footprints in the snow

The doll spilled from his shopping bag
It grinned at him from its box
Dimpled cheeks
Arms spread wide in welcome
And he painted it red
Tacky, sticky, meaty, red

All that Anna wanted for Christmas
was that doll
A Cabbage Patch doll
It had been worth the crowds
And the traffic
Fighting the other shoppers
Bribing the store clerk

For the very last one

Tom had hugged the doll close
Fighting his way through angry shoppers
He had cheated
He hadn't waited in line
They had all seen it
He was rich
Privileged
He could have anything
Take anything he wanted
He opened his wallet
and all the rules bent for him
It wasn't fair

The man with the hard eyes
Like shards of glass
Skin like leather
Smiling without mirth
Watching Tom as he left
Following him into the parking lot

"What the fuck do you want?"

He answered with a flash of metal
Cold and hard
Like his eyes
Stainless steel
winter cold
Sliding between Tom's ribs
Stabbing up into his intestines
Ripping open his belly
His guts unspooled
like thick purple and red slugs
spilling out into the snow

Another flash of steel
Cutting into his neck
Slicing his hands
And arms
And chest
And stabbing
And stabbing
And stabbing
And the man's eyes never changed
Those hard eyes
like shards of glass
never changed
Doll's eyes
Like the Cabbage Patch doll
The last one
For Anna
For Christmas
All red now
red slush

And all the red poured out of Tom's shoes
And out of his pants
As he was dragged into the van
Leaving red trails in the snow
Leaving Anna's doll
The last one
Alone in the snow
Painted red
A gift
For some other little girl

# OWNERSHIP

I purchase your screams
with my steady exertion
my violent effort
rewarded by your sweet fear
each time I hurt you
I feel your joy rise like song
I control the beat

You ride endorphins
to a shivering rapture
your twinkling eyes glaze
and I almost orgasm
my erection throbs
but I am satiated
by your luscious agony

# THE MURDERER YOU WANTED

You love the horror
watching graphic violence
safe in suburban sameness
instead of chained up helpless
captive to my lusts
You imagine knives
cutting and ripping your flesh
chainsaws and axes
Every torture you have seen
on the silver screen
is running through your mind now
you are the scream queen
and I must play my part too
our own slasher flick
for an audience of two
I know I am not
the murderer you wanted
but I want to try
Jason, Michael, and Freddy,
competing for your fear
I pause

hesitate
performance anxiety
I want perfection
I want to earn your terror
to deserve your fear
when I bite down on your throat
you don't even scream
your blood erupts from your neck
you share my embarrassment
it is much too soon
I feel your disappointment
I am ashamed
I refuse to let your death
be one more failure
then
when I start the chainsaw
rip it across you
I see your pain and your fear
And know
I have been redeemed

# THE DEATH THROES OF SUMMER

Autumn came with open arteries
Summer gasped
Its dying breath
And all the trees bled out
Gushing like rainwater
The wool fell from his legs
The last sip of wine
Drooled from his blackening lips
And turned the fields brown
With rotting fruit
The cup spilled from his hand
His horns withdrew
Like a shriveling erection
Shocked into retreat
The music screeched
Like injured children
Abused into pre-maturity
The seductive moist lip smile
Fell to a hard line
on the whore's face

as the last
satyr
died

# HUMANITY

Scraps of meat and bone
haphazardly assembled
to parody gods

Together we rot
drawn together in torment
maggots on a corpse

our imprisoned smiles
in bondage to yesterday
a screaming rictus
masking our pain with humor
our stupidity with art

# THIS CRUEL JOY

Amidst this cruel joy
I remorse while enraptured
that this perfect day
will see its blood spilled by night

For never has life
made anything so perfect
its beauty was not
each day slowly devoured

Your sweet bloody smile
hides your sad certain decay
when the midnight I now fear
is our last refuge from day

That your flawless love
an ephemeral vampire
shall soon melt away
in time's cold holy waters

# BLEEDING FOR YOU

I opened every vein I could reach
exsanguinated in strawberry red pools
to feed your endless thirst
became your living
bleeding
Giving Tree
You emptied me.
I murdered all the others
trying to satiate your hunger
yet your stomach still growls
and my blood
is not enough

# HAUNTED

I awake with a start
each morning
to the sound of thunderous footsteps
slamming doors
cries of rage
bitter sighs
flashing lights
fill the room
the cacophony intensifies
I am surrounded
by anger and sorrow
I want to scream
flee
kill
I am trapped
Hounded
Haunted
possessed
Cannot escape
The din of madness
follows me

# MAKE LOVE TO ME

Make love to me
I want to scream in the lascivious agonies
of your love

Burn me alive
in the voluptuous heat
of your eyes

Shatter my skull
With the ballistic speed
of your tongue

Make Love to Me

I want to perish
impaled on your tongue

I want to drown
in your desires

I want to sacrifice myself

on the altar
of your sex

I want to die
in the gleam
of your eyes

# ONE THOUSAND

If I could sire a thousand vampires
enslave a thousand souls
reanimate a thousand corpses
it would still not make me whole

Fly to a thousand stars
bring them burning back to earth
kill a thousand gods
it would still not prove my worth

A thousand dreams I've lost
A thousand lovers scorned
A thousand paths I've crossed
A thousand bridges burned

I would lead a thousand demons
lay siege at heaven's gate
for one in a thousand angels
eternally I'd wait

For one in a thousand moments

a one in a thousand chance
to take that one sweet angel
for that one final dance

Then I could leave this life appeased
leaving my soul with her
my poor loving heart deceased
like a thousand men before

# YESTERDAY'S ALTAR

The past's a virgin
sacrificed to tomorrow
Its blood feeds demons

# INSOMNIA

One more day in hell
I dread the morning
as those who live in the light
dread the setting sun
the cacophonous din of life
bustling anxious and dreadful
in every corner and crevice
begging hands and greedy mouths
questing eyes
wanting and imploring
every life a responsibility
an obligation
a duty
if I could make it all cease
quiet every heartbeat
stop every breath
then perhaps
I might sleep
again

# MEMORIES

Fossilized seconds whose tracks lead us only to partial remains
where not even their skeletons remain in evidence
Fading photographs yellowing with nostalgia
the mausoleums in which true experience lies inert
as each moment heaps another corpse upon the slab

Experiences that we can never touch
hold against us
feel the gentle warmth of
let bleed down our chests in long salacious rivulets
lick from smooth voluptuous thighs

Experiences with no mass
displace no air
do not crunch broken glass
echo when screamed at
or leave their impressions in the sheets

too much like believing in Christ
too much like believing I love you's

I would like them much better
if I had to clear a space for them
If I could open the closet
and discard the ones I no longer have a use for
If I could taste them
feel them
throw them in the air
catch them in my
two hands
shatter them against the wall
and rub their fragments over my body
until they stuck

... and formed armor

# SYMPATHY FOR FRANKENSTEIN

Watching as it rots
as everything lovely dies
I do understand
wanting to revive the dead
cheat oblivion
reanimate lost passions
expired and mourned

All I want is what I had
And I held heaven once
I would raise a graveyard for it
to hold it again
kiss life back into its carcass
in lightning and fury
I share his dark obsession
My sympathies for Frankenstein

# BEAUTIFUL DEMONS

Mockeries of humanity
made to shame creation
my nightmares
masquerading in flesh
a kaleidoscopic stew of souls
a patchwork tapestry of sins
rapturous agonies
blasphemous unnatural pleasures
shambling through the shadows
between thoughts and actions
whispering my shames and regrets
in the language of the senses

I will not slay my demons
No matter how sharp their claws
How venomous their bite
I will bite back the screams
allow myself to be unmade
so I might be reborn

# SOMETIMES

Love is so profound
You have to hurt to feel it
A bite
A spank
my hand around your throat
Is how you know
you're special
A crack
A lash
a stroke from my cane
Is more intimate than a kiss
A bruise
a welt
a slowly healing cut
Is all the jewelry
that you need
Your moans
Your screams
A safeword never spoken
And I forget there was life
before you

# ABOUT THE AUTHOR

WRATH JAMES WHITE is a former World Class Heavy-weight Kickboxer, a professional Kickboxing and Mixed Martial Arts trainer, distance runner, performance artist, and former street brawler, who is now known for creating some of the most disturbing works of fiction in print.

Wrath is the author of such extreme horror classics as THE RESURRECTIONIST (now a major motion picture titled "Come Back To Me") SUCCULENT PREY, and it's sequel PREY DRIVE, YACCUB'S CURSE, 400 DAYS OF OPPRESSION, SACRIFICE, VORACIOUS, TO THE DEATH, THE REAPER, SKINZZ, EVERYONE DIES FAMOUS IN A SMALL TOWN, THE BOOK OF A THOUSAND SINS, HIS PAIN, POPULATION ZERO and many others. He is the co-author of TERATOLOGIST co-written with the king of extreme horror, Edward Lee, SOME-THING TERRIBLE co-written with his son Sultan Z. White, ORGY OF SOULS co-written with Maurice Broaddus, HERO and THE KILLINGS both co-written with J.F. Gonzalez, POISONING EROS co-written with Monica J. O'Rourke, among others.

Wrath lives and works in Austin, Texas with his three daughters, Isis, Nala, and Zoe, his son and co-author, Sultan Z. White, and his beautiful wife Tammy.